D0088892

Floop
in the Dark

Text by Carole Tremblay
Illustrations by Steve Beshwaty

an imprint of
WINDMILL BOOKS
New York

Published in 2010 by Windmill Books, LLC
303 Park Avenue South, Suite # 1280, New York, NY 10010-3657

Adaptations to North American Edition © 2010 Windmill Books

Original title: Floop dans le noir
Original Publisher: Les éditions Imagine inc
© Carole Tremblay / Steve Beshwaty 2006
© Les éditions Imagine inc. 2006
English text © Les éditions Imagine inc 2006

Text by Carole Tremblay
Illustrations by Steve Beshwaty

Publisher Cataloging in Publication

Tremblay, Carole, 1959-
         Floop in the dark / text by Carole Tremblay ; illustrations by Steve Beshwaty.
p. cm. – (Floop)
Summary: When Floop is awakened by a noise in his bedroom he imagines all the scary creatures that might be lurking in the dark around his bed.
ISBN 978-1-60754-341-1 (lib.) – ISBN 978-1-60754-342-8 (pbk.)
ISBN 978-1-60754-343-5 (6-pack)
1. Fear of the dark—Juvenile fiction   2. Night—Juvenile fiction
3. Monsters—Juvenile fiction   4. Sleep—Juvenile fiction   [1. Fear of the dark—Fiction   2. Night—Fiction   3. Monsters—Fiction   4. Sleep—Fiction]   I. Beshwaty, Steve   II. Title   III. Series
         [E]—dc22

Printed in the United States of America

Floop is asleep.

He is having pleasant dreams that make him smile.

Suddenly . . . clunk! A noise wakes him up.

Floop opens his eyes, but he can't see
anything. It's too dark.

Even though he can't see anything there, he's
convinced he heard something.

Floop doesn't like noises in the night. And he
certainly doesn't like the dark!

He doesn't know what is hiding in the dark.

There could be a **monster** in the dark.

There could be an ogre with big teeth.

There could be a **witch** with a crooked nose.

Or a **vampire** who wants to bite his toe. Or his ear!

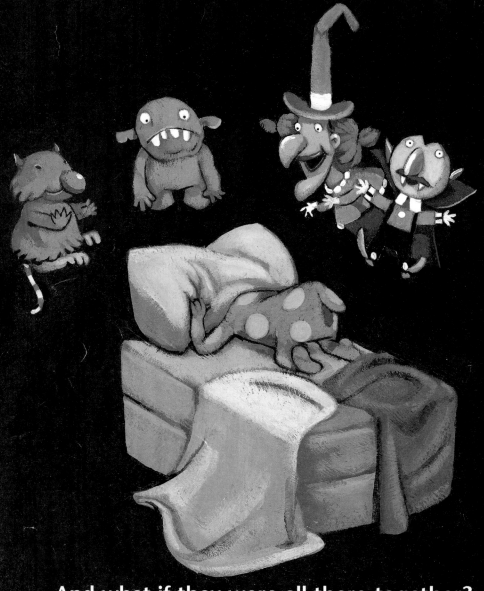

And what if they were all there together?

Oh no! There are a lot of creatures in the dark!

How can Floop get rid of them?

Floop has an idea.

Click! He turns on the lights.

All the creatures disappear.
They are all gone, even the vampire.

It's only Little Bob and he's crying.

What's wrong, Little Bob?

Did Little Bob fall while climbing the shelves?
That must have been the noise Floop heard!

Floop helps Little Bob into bed with him.

Floop and Little Bob quickly fall back asleep.
They must be having sweet dreams now!